Sink or Swim?

First published in 2008
by Wayland

Text copyright © Pippa Goodhart 2008
Illustration copyright © Sue Mason 2008

Wayland
338 Euston Road
London NW1 3BH

Wayland Australia
Level 17/207 Kent Street
Sydney, NSW 2000

Series Editor: Louise John
Editor: Katie Powell
Cover design: Paul Cherrill
Design: D.R.ink
Consultant: Shirley Bickler

A CIP catalogue record for this book is available from the British Library.

ISBN 9780750255264

Printed in China

Wayland is a division of Hachette Children's Books,
an Hachette Livre UK company

www.hachettelivre.co.uk

Sink or Swim?

Written by Pippa Goodhart
Illustrated by Sue Mason

WAYLAND

The class was going swimming.

The bus came to collect
the children.

"Jump on, everyone," said
Miss Samson. "No messing
about now."

"I don't want to go,"
said Jake.

"Come on, Jake!" said Bella.

"Swimming is fun,"
said Nasim.

At the pool the children
got ready.

"I'm going to swim like
a fish!" said Nasim.

"I'm going to splash like
a hippo!" said Bella.

"I don't want to swim at all,"
said Jake.

"Hurry up, Jake," said Miss Samson.

"I don't like swimming,"
said Jake.

"Just get ready, Jake,"
said Miss Samson.

13

"OK, everyone. In you get!"
said the swimming teacher.

"I don't like swimming,"
said Jake. "I'll sink."

"Don't be silly, Jake. Get in the pool!" said Miss Samson.

"I don't like swimming. The water will be cold," he said.

Jake sat on the side and watched his friends.

Nasim swam like a fish.

Bella splashed like a hippo.
"Well done, Bella!" said Miss
Samson. "Keep going!"

21

"Let's get into teams and play a game of water ball," said the swimming teacher. "Where's the ball?"

22

"Here it is!" said Jake.
He threw the ball to
the teacher.

24

"Come on, Jake!" said
Miss Samson. "Your team
needs you."

Jake liked playing water ball.
He liked it a lot.

He dipped his big toe into
the water.

It felt nice and warm.

"Jake! Look!" shouted Bella suddenly.

The ball was flying towards the goal.

Jake jumped in and caught it just in time.

Jake's team clapped
and cheered.

"What a save!" shouted Bella and Nasim.

Jake smiled. "I think I like swimming after all!"

START READING is a series of highly enjoyable books for beginner readers. **The books have been carefully graded to match the Book Bands widely used in schools.** This enables readers to be sure they choose books that match their own reading ability.

Look out for the Band colour on the book in our Start Reading logo.

The Bands are:

🔵	Pink Band 1
🔵	Red Band 2
🔵	Yellow Band 3
🔵	Blue Band 4
🔵	Green Band 5
🔵	Orange Band 6
🔵	Turquoise Band 7
🔵	Purple Band 8
🔵	Gold Band 9

START READING books can be read independently or shared with an adult. They promote the enjoyment of reading through satisfying stories supported by fun illustrations.

Pippa Goodhart lives with her husband, three daughters, a dog, a cat and four chickens who all leave interesting footprints on her floors. She found learning to read hard, but now loves reading, and writing, books.

Sue Mason grew up in East Sussex, surrounded by trees, eating crumpets. She illustrates from a happy little studio called The Chocolate Factory, which she shares with special friends. Sometimes they break from work to have a little dance around and eat cake.